A SHOCKINGLY SHORT
HISTORY OF
ABSOLUTELY EVERYTHING

JOHN FARMAN was made in Britain just after the war. He was raised and educated (pause for laughter) in the north of London, moving later to the middle bit where he studied illustration (pause for more laughter) at the Royal College of Art. He has two children, no wife and a goldfish called Colin and lives in an ex-asylum within spitting distance of a high-security prison. Need we say more.

A SHOCKINGLY SHORT
HISTORY OF
ABSOLUTELY EVERYTHING

by

John Farman

(*who also drew the pictures*)

MACMILLAN

First published 1996 by Macmillan Children's Books
a division of Macmillan Publishers Limited
25 Eccleston Place, London SW1W 9NF
and Basingstoke

Associated companies throughout the world

ISBN 0 330 34904 X

Text and illustrations copyright © John Farman 1996

The right of John Farman to be identified as the
author of this work has been asserted by him in
accordance with the Copyright, Designs and Patents Act 1988.

1 3 5 7 9 8 6 4 2

A CIP catalogue record for this book is available from
the British Library.

Printed by Mackays of Chatham PLC, Kent

For Colin

Contents

· ·

Before we start . . .

Nobody in their right mind would attempt to write the history of absolutely everything, which, apparently, is why my publishers asked me. Knowing that I come from the Get Home Early School of Book Writing, they seemed fairly sure it would only take me a few months. Sadly, it didn't.*

History's a funny old subject. What's important to some people just isn't to others. For instance, my editor told me, rather peevishly, that I'd forgotten to mention the invention of electricity. Look I'm sorry but SO WATT (electrical joke). After all, you could hardly say it's had any great influence on the twentieth century (blast – my wo

rd pr oce sso r s e em s to be pl a y ing u p).

That's better – just a loose connection. Now where was I? Ah yes, I was talking about what's important. As you will realize, I had to do quite a lot of shortening to get absolutely everything in (otherwise this book would be at least twice the length). If, by any remote chance, I've left anything else out (apart from Shakespeare and electricity) please write to me and let me know what it is in full detail.

On second thoughts, write to my publishers.

* It didn't take nearly that long.

THE VERY BEGINNING

The Very Beginning

· ·

Around five million years ago, before monkeys even thought about standing up for themselves and being proper men, life was relatively simple and straightforward. If you can imagine knowing absolutely nothing (which, believe it or not, is quite hard) then it must have followed that there should be absolutely nothing to worry about.

They didn't, for instance, realize that the world could be anything but flat, that the sun was anything other than a yellow football (not that they knew what footballs were), and that television, telegraphs and telephone communication via an orbiting satellite would be arriving shortly... ish. Concepts like life after death, God (or even Cliff Richard) were thousands of years away, so all that was required of them was to find enough for themselves to eat, whilst making quite sure they didn't become food for anything (or anyone) else. This ruled out the need to pass exams or driving tests, earn a living or take out insurance policies or expensive mortgages. As for all the other bits and pieces that keep modern man, and his female counterpart, awake at night (apart from one) – forget it, they simply took what was going.

Then, one day, one of our apecestors discovered that if you were to bash a soft thing with a hard thing, it tended to fall over. The first soft things were rather dim-witted subspecies (later called ANIMALS), which he fancied for supper or, more probably, one of the female cavepersons whom he simply fancied. The first hard things were usually clubs of a wood or stone nature or simply stones of a rock nature (?).

Walkie Talkie

Three million years later, when his brain had doubled in size, he became fully 'erectus' (no jokes – pleease!!). Standing up was a bit of a breakthrough. Admittedly, it slowed him (and her) down when running – monkeys can still run twice as fast as us – but the added height meant that instead of grovelling around in the dust, they could look over the grass (unmown) and search much further afield for something to eat (or hopefully catch sight of something that was about to eat them!). They didn't smell very good (or should that be very *well?*) so their eyesight was their greatest defence. Not only that, but it freed their hands to do other things, like swing amongst trees, pluck leaves and carry things. Having their hands free also meant that they could have a bash at all sorts of new crafts like making bowls and egg-cups out of mud or

shaping quite-hard things with very-hard things to make tools and jolly-sharp weapons: they had accidentally invented TECHNOLOGY (and CROCKERY).

Tune Time

It was probably when Homo Erectus was hitting things with other things that he noticed that they made different noises. By striking them in a certain order he found that sound patterns emerged causing Mrs Erectus and their growing family and friends to jig up and down (later known as DANCE). Although far from composing a symphony he had inadvertently made the first MUSIC and, unfortunately, the first xylophone (no pain – no gain!). Later he got the hang of blowing down long, hollow things making odd whooshy noises. If only he'd known he'd stumbled upon the prototype of the didgeri-doo (which in turn led to the prototype of Rolf Harris) I reckon he'd have thrown them away fairly smartish.

The Big Heat

Mr and Mrs Homo Erectus, unlike their creepy-crawly rellies, refused to stop evolving and, when finding their equipment slightly inadequate for the new tasks they set themselves, traded themselves in, becoming the highly improved Homo Sapiens – meaning 'wise man'.

'How's about lighting a fire, dear?' Mrs Sapiens asked innocently one chilly morn (she didn't think it nice to call him Homo). Mr Sapiens realized that, whatever fire was, it hadn't been invented yet, and smashed his newish flint axe against an oldish rock in a fit of pique, causing the first single spark (and the beginning of SCIENCE). Unfortunately, the local fire engine was still awaiting the wheel (or four) to be developed and the ensuing conflagration (fire, to you!), though having the desired effect warmth-wise, destroyed a forest covering the best part of the continent.

Nonetheless, the world 600,000 years ago, especially in the West, was getting colder and colder, and the Sapiens (and their kids) soon realized that they simply weren't hairy enough to keep warm.

'I'm still freezing,' Mrs Sapiens screamed, huddled round what was left of the great fire.

'What d'you expect me to do about it?' her long-suffering old man grunted, as snow began to swirl around the cave.

Nothing to Wear

Mrs Sapiens, ingenious as ever, promptly sent him out to nick the skins off the more furry (and less speedy) of the subspecies and then set about running up neat little outfits for the family. The lady next-entrance (doors hadn't been invented) peeked over the prototype fence jealously and rushed home to make a more stylish version. It was probably her fault that the FASHION business was born.

In hot places, like Africa and Australia, people

weren't too fussed about clothing, and had rather neatly turned black as a protection from the sun. But human nature being human nature, they soon wanted to find a way of looking different from their neighbours so started daubing their bodies in bright colours. Little did they know that they'd kicked off the multi-million pound COSMETICS industry.

Home Improvements

Mrs Sapiens never gave up harassing her partner, however (having recently discovered the joys of NAGGING) and was soon looking round the family home to see if it could be cheered up or modernized in any way.

'When are you going to do something about this blasted cave?' she cried, pointing at their dingy, soot-blackened surroundings.

'What can I do about it?' replied hubby, lounging around waiting for telly or the Sunday Sport to be invented.

'What we need is wallpaper!'

But the poor chap had never *heard* of walls, let alone paper (let alone DIY) so instead, he mixed up different coloured muds and drew rather silly pictures of all the dumb animals and the even dumber fellow men he'd slaughtered lately. Mrs Sapiens, though far from happy (preferring something along prettier, more floral lines), realized that her old man had made some ART and was almost proud.

Grow Your Own

Then, a mere 10,000 years ago, our hero (and his Mrs) went into the hunting and gathering business, on account of having chewed up and swallowed just about everything edible for miles. After sticking this for a few thousand years, they (his descendants, that is!) found all the walking and running too much like hard work and grouped together with all their fellow hunter-gatherers and became stay-at-homers. They then invented AGRICULTURE by sneakily befriending the local beasts and plants, rendering both animals and vegetables alike far easier to catch. They

FIRST PETS

← EARLY BIRD

DOES THIS MEAN HE WON'T EAT US?

did, however, spare some of the animals, like dogs, budgies and gerbils, and allowed them to hang around the hut. They had, by pure chance, discovered PETS.

Then one morning, 5,000 years ago, a Ukrainian guy realized that a horse could trot along almost as well with him on its back as without. When he found that riding this beast made moving from place to place far less tiring (for him) and considerably faster – he decided, on balance, not to eat it. TRANSPORT was born.

Village life

After another couple of thousand years, these small groups began to grow quite large and what started as handfuls of mud huts grew into new-fangled villages and then towns. The great advantage of having a settled place to live was that you didn't have to cart all your possessions around wherever you went. The downside was that you had loads of neighbours. It probably wasn't long before someone (probably called Jones) wanted a bigger and better mud hut than everybody else, and promptly set about designing it. This became the rudimentary beginnings of ARCHITECTURE.

Although SHOPS as such weren't quite invented, the very first thing ever written (or the earliest ever found) was in the form of a shopping list, scratched on a piece of clay, which appears to have been jotted down at a place called

Uruk in the fertile bit between the Tigris and Euphrates rivers. Admittedly, half a dozen eggs, a pint of milk, a small sliced loaf and a jar of Marmite were not exactly *War and Peace*, but this document obviously led to something we now call LITERATURE.

It was also probably around this time that the first rather nosy person asked a friend what was on his mind, what life was all about, and where he came from (man!). This thinking about thinking about thinking grew into what we now call PHILOSOPHY.

So there we have it. Mankind was up and running, and the scene was set for his development. He could cultivate his own food, design his own clothes, knock up things to make his domestic life easier, build dwellings to suit his and his family's needs, investigate how the world around him worked, draw and write about what he found out, travel further afield and think and talk about what he thought he was thinking and talking about.

QUITE SOON AFTER THAT

Quite Soon After That

. . . .

Around 4500 BC, while we were still grovelling around being rather primitive over in the West, CIVILIZATIONS, as such, were forming everywhere else (like the East). To qualify as a fully paid-up 'civilization' meant that the people involved must have developed methods of farming, a system of writing, some sort of government and usually a handful of gods to bow down and sacrifice themselves (or their goats and families) to.

At last the world was beginning to fall into definable regions. As early maps were a bit hit and miss GEOGRAPHY becomes a little tricky to describe with any degree of accuracy. For example, the British Isles, according to Roman cartographers (map-makers, that is), were teetering on the edge of the world, while the Arabs confused everyone by putting the south at the top and the north at the bottom. The ancient Indians, it has to be said, were no use at all at maps as, for a start, they believed the world rested on the back of a turtle, which doesn't bode that well for the more detailed bits.

What Day is It?

Nobody could tell the time in those days, but they could count the days, so, in 4241 BC, some clever Egyptian, bored with never being able to plan ahead for a barbecue, execution or pyramid opening (or should that be closing?), sat down and invented a CALENDAR a bit like the one we still use today (days, months, years etc). The Jews, always guaranteed to do something different, followed 500 years later with their own.

In Mesopotamia, some of the mud towns that had grown from the first mud villages (that had grown from the first mud huts), joined together to be the first mud cities (like Babylon). But it was the Sumerians who had the greatest influence over the Mediterranean regions of Asia. They invented proper writing, learned how to add up, finally thought up the brilliant idea of putting wheels on the four corners of their carts (using the spare wheel to throw pots on), and made dinky little lamps that ran on fat (from melted-down animals); They also had ships, but these weren't as fab or as numerous as those of the Cretans, who invented proper TRADE by whizzing around all over the Mediterranean flogging their gear to anyone who was interested.

The Game's Up

Throughout the world it was dawning on people that fighting could be good fun just to watch, without actually being involved or – more to the point – hurt. Wrestling, therefore, became the very first organized SPORT, though I doubt it was anything like the pantomime we see on telly these days. Talking of early sports, ancient carvings (found in Norway of all places) indicate that even then winter sports like skiing were all the rage. Après-ski, however, came some time – er – 'après'.

Keep-fit or aerobics (pretentious or what?) didn't arrive for thousands of years, as most folks in those pre-car, pre-bus, pre-train (pre-heart-attack!) days had to walk miles to get anywhere and didn't sit for hours every night in front of an illuminated box (eating TV cholesterol-enhanced dinners).

Mine's a Pint!

Around that time, some bright spark up Babylon way discovered something that was to influence history to this day. Something that has caused practically more strife, more sickness (especially on Friday nights), has broken up more marriages and given more pleasure, especially to men, than practically everything else... BEER!

Slightly less contentious, but almost as catastrophic, the Sumerians replaced barley as their currency and invented the root of all evil – MONEY, in the form of little metal coins.

By around 3000 BC all the Egyptians who weren't farmers (which was about twelve) were becoming quite cultured. They filled their leisure time by painting, weaving and playing music. Being fine craftsmen, they soon had enough instruments for a small band. They'd had harps and flutes for some time but they then added lyres (a sort of naff cross between a harp and a guitar) and whopping great clarinets: drums and clangy things didn't pitch up for another couple of thousand years. Had they had any chums in China they could also have added a couple of bamboo pipes (which had just been invented) to their combo, and a little later (2500 BC) could have written the tunes down, as those clever Chinese had just worked out a way of doing it.

Art Goes Big

The biggest deal art-wise was a vast sculpture at Giza (Egypt) of some geezer called Sphinx who was mostly lion with a man's head on top (with a silly hat on top of that). The Egyptians had become rather good at drawing, but only if you like the aforementioned creatures with mixed-up heads and bodies, people with two left feet and landscapes that look as if they've been treated to a cosmic steamroller. The only records we have of this were found in their huge, new pointy tombs called pyramids, in which they buried their mummies (presumably their daddies were chucked in a sand pit).

What's Up, Doc?

But how did they deal with sick people in ancient days? In pre-historic times MEDICINE, as such, didn't exist. If you were feeling a little dicky, whatever was amiss usually got worse until you were ex. This seems a trifle tough, but like all things, if you didn't know any better, you'd jolly well learn to live (or die) with it. The Sumerians were about the first people not to stare dejectedly at their ill people and reach for the nearest spade. They began, when not wailing to their gods, to investigate the medical properties of mineral water and plants. It's interesting to note (well, fairly) that a lot of the stuff they used then is still used today.

By the time the Israelites, led by their main man Moses, were a-crossing the Jordan in 1250 BC, the whole world was in ferment and civilizations and empires were being swapped around like a rock star's groupies. Inventions and things-to-make-life-better were two-a-penny, and brilliant new diseases like leprosy were all the rage in places like Egypt and India. Even Denmark came into the picture with, would you believe, the first trumpet, though I suppose no one knew how to play it (and it's arguable whether it has ever made anyone's life better). The Scots, I'm happy to relate, did finally manage to invent something besides the almost inedible haggis, even if it was very small. How odd that a nation that insisted on everyone wearing skirts is responsible for the common or garden 'button'.

It's All Greek

It was the Greeks, however, in the first century BC, who cornered the market in the 'how-does-it-all-work' or philosophy department. It's not that they were the very first to think of these things, but they did have the common sense to write it down. This became known as the Classical Era. It started with a guy called Thales of Miletus who began by asking what the universe was made of. He kicked off by claiming that everything (including himself) was made of water, but this was regarded as rather wet by a whole host of phollowing philosophers who suggested that the stuff they were all looking for was anything from fire (Heraclitus), to air (Anaximenes), to slime (Anaximander).

Eventually Democritus (another Greek) came up with the daftest idea of all: that everything in the universe from a pig to a pyramid was made up of tiny little particles called *atoms*, and that these little chaps whiz around in space looking for others to join up with and make things. Even he couldn't have known how close to the truth he was.

How does it all work?

Hippocrates (him of Hippocratic Oath fame) told all the gods (pre our god – God) that from now on (460 BC), thanks all the same, he and his fellow doctors would be in sole charge of making people better.

Most famous of all was Aristotle (yet another Greek), who founded LOGIC, PHYSICS, BIOLOGY, the HUMANITIES and MUSICAL THEORY when he wasn't teaching a nipper called

Alexander how to be Great.*

Archimedes (yes! Greek too) was dead clever, but a bit weird. He was the guy that invented STREAKING, when he dashed, damp but delirious, through the streets of Syracuse, stark-naked, having accidentally tripped over the

laws of water displacement (and a bar of soap) while climbing into the bath. This discovery became rather useful when designing ships (and rubber ducks).

OK that's enough Greeks for now! Suffice to say that

*Alexander III of Macedon did indeed become 'Great', taking only thirteen years to create an Empire.

they certainly weren't behind the Acropolis door when brains were handed out, and they were the only lads (there were no women, honest!) to attempt the big questions like 'What is air?', 'Where does space end?', 'How does our body work?' or 'Why do chickens cross the road?' The biggest brain-teasers of all, however, were: 'What is Earth?' and 'Where exactly is it?' They eventually chose old Aristotle's version which claimed that we earthlings were at the centre of the universe and that everything revolved round us (à la Princess Di); a version that topped the charts for hundred of years. Shame it was completely wrong!

Play Up

Not much to report on the Greek music front, I'm afraid. It seems that apart from singing daft odes to each other about their somewhat eccentric gods, the Greeks hadn't gone in much for pushing the bounds of musical development further, apart from having trumpet competitions (which sounds to me like a positive move backwards). The Chinese were probably playing the same plinky-plonky stuff as they are today, while the Scandinavians were, even then, trying to write something that wouldn't eventually come last in the Eurovision Song Contest. As for Britain – forget it. The crude Celts were far too busy keeping a watchful eye on those blasted Romans to worry about that sort of business.

Back to the Greeks

The Greeks loved being competitive and were therefore big on board games (Serpentus and Ladderus?), ball games (crickitus boringus...), as well as inventing ATHLETICS. Sports like running, jumping, running-and-jumping-at-the-same-time, spear throwing (javelin) or ice skating (not really!) were extremely popular. Plate or discus throwing still remains as a quaint custom in many Greek restaurants, though the javelin is somewhat frowned on (unless used for kebabs). The development of all the flash (if somewhat poncy) athletic gear came much later, as Greek athletes wore nothing apart from olive wreaths to keep their hair (yes, their hair!) from bouncing around when they ran.

The Romans eventually put a stop to all that silly science and thinking, being far more interested in conquering and having a good time. They were originally a group of rough, tough farmers who lived in the hills overlooking the River Tiber. One day one of them suggested that they all pull together and create a big town (Rome) and a brand new empire (The Roman). And didn't they do well? Several hundred years later they'd taken over most of the countries surrounding the Mediterranean and had even nabbed England off the Celts.

Jesus at Last

Everyone must have had an inkling that Jesus was coming because all the dates before his birth were followed by BC (*Before Christ*). Afterwards they preceded all the dates with AD – which stands for *Anno Domini*. (Personally, I'd have put AC as in *After Christ*, but *Anno Domini* means the same sort of thing, *In the Year of our Lord*, and anyway nobody asked me.)

Science was still popular, but by now many of the earth's mysteries had been discovered. Pliney the Elder (a much later Greek), seeing the way things were going, thought it might be a neat idea to jot them all down in actual writing, and scribbled all that was currently known (and a fair bit that wasn't!) about astronomy, geography, tautology and zoology, cramming it into 37 volumes (finished in AD 59). All the other 'onomies' and 'ologies' lined up in the 'yet-to-be invented' queue.

Science-wise, the Greeks had been extremely good news, but as I said before, the Romans never seemed that interested in the stuff that the Greeks had so conscientiously started, being far more interested in building roads to take their conquering further afield and building brill buildings and arenas in which to feed their slaves to their lions and have orgies in.

The crunch came about in AD 529, when the Roman Emperor Justinian, who wasn't big on knowledge,

boarded up the Academy and Lyceum in Athens (flash schools of science and ballroom-dancing) and destroyed the museum in Alexandria, preferring to concentrate on inventing stuff like central heating and baths to jolly up the Romans' already jolly lifestyles. Having said that, lots of useful things were invented or developed during this period: a proper 365 day calendar in India, a sundial in Newcastle (sun in Newcastle?), windmills in Persia, bombs and wheelbarrows (to carry them in?) in China, spectacles in Florence and toothpaste in Rome – to name but a few.

... and America

If you're wondering what was going on over on the American continent – fret not! It had been getting along quite happily without the rest of the world and had originally been populated by a bunch of Asian hunter-gatherers who'd strolled across the land-bridge that joined the two huge land masses, before being cut off when the ice melted after the last Ice Age (rendering them well and truly in-continent). Soon the postcards stopped arriving from the folks back home and the Asians spread throughout North and Middle America, content to hunt and gather at will dressed as Red Indians. The first proper civilization occurred way down south of Mexico, where a bunch called the Mayans built fab cities in their own quirky style, blissfully unaware that anyone else existed.

... and Australia

As for Australia, the indigenous Aborigines were so cut off after their personal land connection with South East Asia flooded over, that they didn't really have to think much about anything until they were discovered and overrun by tourists and convicts in the last couple of hundred years. As for culture, many would have it that Australia's still waiting.

Hello Darkness

But the Golden Age, which had seen such mighty leaps forward in our knowledge and perception of the world, was becoming somewhat tarnished. By about the fifth century, the light was growing dim throughout the western world and it was time for the Dark Ages.

THE MIDDLE BIT

The Middle Bit

. . . .

The Dark Ages

Let's see briefly what was going on in the world during the years leading up to AD 1000. After years of occupation the English saw the Romans pack their suitcases and row home to Italy for some decent food. They'd obviously come to the conclusion that as far as conquering was concerned, Britain simply wasn't worth the effort (damned cheek!). In fact, the poor dears were going through what turned out to be much more than just a sticky patch: shortly afterwards the whole of the western bit of the Roman Empire, having declined for ages, promptly fell – to a mixture of beastly Barbarians, fearful Franks, ghastly Goths and various vicious Vandals.

A little later, when Attila the head-Hun died, his horrid under-Huns were forced out of Europe, never to be heard of again. Most sensational and devastating of all, the savage Saxons captured – wait for it – Pevensy, a village on the Sussex coast. It was as though the western

world was turning into a massive car boot sale, with whole
nations (and villages) changing hands once-a-fortnight.

Science Dies

Proper science may have come to a dead end, but a fab
new craze involving a mixture of dodgy science and even
dodgier magic was invented and called ALCHEMY. This
was the two basic (and dumb) pursuits of a) finding
the philosophers' stone – a substance that would turn
anything put next to it into gold (like fish?) – and b) the
Elixir of Life – a rather snazzy beverage which would keep
you fit and alive for ever (medieval Lucozade?).

But to be perfectly honest, the Church had put such a kibosh on anything vaguely progressive (or that involved smiling) that there's very little to report for the next 500 years or so — ah yes — apart from mere details like the population being halved by various plagues and epidemics (no doubt because they didn't wash their hands after going to the loo); the Pope-of-the-day sending a trainee saint (Mr Augustine) over to see if there was any business to be done in Britain; a Byzantine Emperor called Maurice (an Emperor called Maurice?) being assassinated; China finding out how to make CHINA (called porcelain); a guy called Rupert becoming another Saint in Austria (before becoming a bear in Nutwood); Fez becoming the capital of Morocco (before becoming a hat); the Irish discovering Iceland (Magnus O'Magnusson?); someone deciding, for some totally perverse and deeply suspect reason, to join the north and south of London by bridge; and the invention of stirrups to protect certain parts of the anatomy (not the horse's) when riding.

Half-time

If you were to try to find a name for the chunk of history that separated the ancient from the modern world, between, say, the years AD 1000 and 1500 you really couldn't do much better than call them the Middle Ages ('cos they were in the middle and did go on for ages!).

Millennium Ahoy

It's interesting to note that whenever the world approaches a millennium (1000, 2000 etc.) there always seems to be a group of people who endeavour to scare the pants off all the others by telling them that the world is going to end. The year 1000 was no exception, and on the 31st of December AD 999 I bet millions of people sat up late, on their extremely best behaviour, thinking that God's imminent judgement would decide whether they'd go up to the Wings and Harp Department, or down for a severe barbecuing!

With hindsight we realize that this was a slight over-reaction, as the only negative thing to happen was an outbreak throughout Europe of a new disease called St Vitus's* Dance. Despite this particular penny dropping, some loonies are *still* drumming up support for the end of the world in the year 2000 – but that's another story.

Here Come the Harolds

35 years later, King Canute (him of damp feet fame), short of a good birthday present, gave England to his boy Harold to play with. Harold was the big name (amongst boys) so it was no surprise that it was another Harold

---

* Patron saint of twitching

(King) who, 31 years later, was well and truly conquered by King Norman the William (is that right?) on an away-day from France, making the English French for quite a long time.

Practically nothing was going on in this half of the world that wasn't to do with God. Nothing, that is, apart from Halley's comet being spotted on its first trip round the block, a Venetian entrepreneur building a daft-looking boat called a gondola, the Chinese playing cards for the first time, Britain pinching chess from somewhere foreign, people blowing their noses into the first hankies and a few less important events like the Turks grabbing most of Asia Minor off the Byzantine army.

Even better, someone somewhere challenged someone else to a race while they were sitting on their horses. Some other person (without a horse) then bet someone completely else (also without a horse) that the first someone would beat the second someone, and suddenly horse-racing and GAMBLING were born.

John the Jerk

Poor King John of England (who was actually horrid) died in 1218, which, although brill news for the English, was sad for him (and his girl Magna Carta), as he missed hearing the first English song 'Sumer is icumen in', and seeing the first giraffes imported. On the other hand, he also missed the Crusaders bringing home leprosy a couple of years later (though for him, it would've been too late to have made much difference).

If you think I'm ignoring all the other peoples and civilizations at this time, I'm sorry, but they all seemed to be fighting each other quite satisfactorily. Genghis Khan (who was – allegedly – politically to the right of Hitler) was busy conquering Persia, and the Mongols were sharpening their spears ready to shake them at Russia.

Plague Time

Time for another nice new plague. In 1349 some touring rats visited England from Europe and, though feeling fine themselves (for rats), infected and sub-sequently put paid to one third of the population with the dreaded Black Death (so called because it turned you black and had a habit of killing you). As it happens, though not really related, tennis had just been invented in England so I suppose having a severely reduced population at least made it a little easier to get a court (it's an ill wind that blows nobody any good). In Germany they were trying their hand at persecuting the Jews, but unfortunately, this time round nobody else seemed to mind.

Science Hits the Middle Ages

Although in the West, alchemy (see p30) had largely replaced all the proper scientific study started by the Greeks, it was a different story throughout the rest of the world, particularly out East where they'd been going it alone. The Chinese, for instance, had discovered the merits of books (and how to print them) which should have made the communication of ideas much easier (if anyone could read).

They used paper, not only for early money and books, but also for far more delicate purposes (as well as blowing their noses!). They told the time by sticking long poles in the ground (gnomons) and measuring the shadows, but found they had a tendency to be late for appointments if the sun went in... In 1090, to get over

this problem, they constructed the first mechanical water-clock in Peking, but found they were always late if the temperature dropped below freezing.

By the fifteenth century the Chinese also found out that coal would burn in their hearths (which sorted out the frozen water-clock problem) and that they could blow each other up with gunpowder, both of which they lit with the first matches. Gunpowder was to turn out quite useful for WARS which were becoming ever so popular.

Arabs Get Top Marks
If the Chinese were good at science, however, the Arabs were even better. There's no doubt that whizzing all over the world wheeler-dealering allowed them to pick up vast tracts of cheap foreign knowledge. But, to be fair, it wasn't just second-hand information that took them to the top. They practically re-invented the astronomy that had lain dormant since the Golden Age of the Greeks, they made huge leaps forward in medicine and they pushed the science of mathematics to new and incalculable (?) heights.

At the Doctor's
Medicine was one of the only sciences to survive the Dark Ages (which, obviously, didn't affect China and Arabia), as the Christians, though seemingly happy to lose the plot

in other areas, were fed up with plagues and epidemics and going to heaven before closing time. But although they'd begun to use herbs and drugs quite freely, there was still a lot of eye-of-serpent, wart-of-toad and other magical mumbo-jumbo involved. Many of the European monks had studied medicine when not praying and making alcoholic drinks and in the ninth century a flash medical school had opened in Salerno in Italy, which was to make Western medicine itself much better.

But it was over in Egypt (Baghdad to be precise) that health care reached its real peak. They had over a thousand licensed doctors, huge hospitals and even loony bi— whoops – mental homes. Unlike the Greeks, however, they were a bit lacking in the old anatomy department, probably due to the fact that chopping up bodies was given the automatic thumbs down by Islamic Law (unless it was for that cruellest cut of all (circumcision) or the removal of the odd thief's hand). It might or might not be worth noting that the very first flu epidemic hit Paris in 1414 – just as the Middle Ages were drawing to a close.

... and Music

Over on this side of the world all you could listen to was rather grumpy and severe church music (chants and stuff) and all that 'hey-nonny-nonny-no' junk that French troubadours performed (avec lute) and the sort of daft ditties that English weirdos like Morris dancers still like to hop about to. The Celts played unrecognizable tunes on instruments with unpronounceable names like crwths, splymthrts and brtyclyupts, while, over in China they went in for enormous squeaky orchestras consisting of flutes, bells, guitars, gongs and drums, that had no harmonies and used a five note scale with no semi-tones or polyphonics. The first attempts at polyphonics (several melodies playing at the same time) weren't heard in Europe until AD 855 but nobody seemed to care what the tunes were and anyway the Pope, realizing it might lead to a certain amount of enjoyment, forbade it.

The first kettle drums and trumpets to hit Europe, by the way, were brought over by Arab door-to-door drum and trumpet salesmen, while a huge 400 pipe organ was being played at Winchester Monastery in the South of England. By 1466, at the end of the Middle Ages, printed music became available, ballet dancing was first seen in Italian courts, and the newish Oxford University began giving degrees in Music (The Three Degrees?).

... and Art

The Chinese were no doubt the best artists throughout the Middle Ages. This wasn't that difficult as over in the West everyone had forgotten how. All that wonderful Greek classical art had either been lost, painted over or simply destroyed, in favour of the sort of stuff you see in that worst (and first) CARTOON strip of all time – the Bayeux Tapestry (in Bayeux). It was as if a whole area of artistic endeavour had ground to a halt on the brow of the hill and was slipping, ever faster, backwards. And it was all the fault of God (or His spokesmen). Luckily, the Chinese knew precious little, and cared even less, about what was going on in the rest of the world (and cared even less than that about God) so carried on developing their simple, swirling uncluttered designs and landscapes, painting scrolls and wall hangings (mostly take-away menus) and decorating fine porcelain.

Time for Temples

Throughout India, Egypt and the Far East flash temples and palaces were still being built, and decorated with fab paintings and sculptures and boundless, beautiful Buddhas. The best we could do over here was in AD 913 when Ethelfleda (Alfred the Great's nipper) piled up a huge earthen mound to put Warwick Castle on. Around AD 1000, however, cathedral mania hit Britain and Europe. Practically every big city tried to outdo its neighbours by making its personal cathedral even bigger and more lavish, and some even got in trendy Italian painters, the best in Europe, to decorate them. Back home, the Italians weren't quite so good at building, however, and were suffering from a spate of cowboy builders, like the ones who forgot the foundations in the now-sinking Venice or threw up that wonky tower in Pisa.

'Ee Signor – I donta know whatta you talk about. Of course eet's straight. I seenk you must 'ave one legga shorter than ze other.'

In 1305 a Florentine painter called Giotto became very well known; firstly, because he found out how to do shading and shadows; and, secondly (and more likely)

because he was one of the first artists to remember to sign his name. He was largely responsible for the revival of an Italian art movement that looked back nostalgically to everything the Greeks had been doing centuries before.

This became the Golden Age of Italian painting, the members of which sound like a Who's Who of anyone who was any good with the old brushes. OK, they only seemed to do long-necked, identically ugly Madonnas (looking remarkably like Boy George) with grumpy little wizened plastic Jesuses and the obligatory handful of fat cherubs flitting about. But they had to start again somewhere.

Perspective

The next big breakthrough came in 1412 when an Italian architect/sculptor called Brunelleschi realized that as things got further away they got smaller (sort of), and that they always seemed to do it in proportion. He worked out a method by which you could represent this in two dimensions, and his theory of perspective (or how to represent distance) was an instant hit amongst all those artists who couldn't work out why their landscapes looked so flat.

Renaissance Time

Just as the whistle was about to blow on the Middle Ages, when Joan of Arc was ready to be grilled in France for being a witch, the terrible Turks were about to conquer

Constantinople (thus ending the Byzantine Empire and starting the Ottoman one), the Incas were setting up home in Peru... a little boy called Leonardo de Finchley was learning how to paint, and an even littler boy, called Christopher, was causing his parents (Mr and Mrs Columbus) a great deal of concern owing to his annoying habit of running away to see... what was round the next headland!

England Fights Itself

In case you think I've forgotton little old England... Our 100 Years War with France ended in 1453 as we cleared out and lost everything except Calais (why Calais?). A little later, the Civil War (to decide whether white roses were better than red ones), was settled in favour of the Tudors, making Edward IV king.

...THE NEXT BIT

... The Next Bit

. . . .

In the last quarter of the fifteenth century those surly Spanish seemed to be taking over the world. In 1492, to prove the point, the now-grown-up Christopher Columbus set off from Palos, Spain, trying to find a way to India which didn't involve going all round the pointy bit at the bottom of Africa. He figured that if he went straight ahead, rather than turning left or right, as everyone had done before, he might get a result. The bad news was that he didn't find India at all (Vasco da Gama did!), but the 'good' news was that he bumped into America instead, claiming it for Spain, and everyone had a drink (sherry) when they realized that there was much more world to exploit than they'd originally thought.

Slaves for Sale

1501 was a black year for black Africans. The Spanish, on another of their all-conquering sail-abouts, noticed that there was an endless supply of people on the African continent who had been happily getting on with their own lives, and hadn't really needed to develop any way of defending themselves. Being short of a workforce in that bit of the West Indies that Columbus had bagged, they put two-and-two together and started kidnapping the poor blighters – so inventing SLAVERY, and later, as a by-product, THE BLUES (see p78).

Henry Again

Back home in England, another little chap called Henry was born; destined to be known as Eighth, to wear that big sparkly hat, to marry lots of unsuitable women, to dispose of them in a rather chauvinist and ungentlemanly manner, and to get excommunicated from the Catholic Church for his trouble. Still, what do kings care? Those are the perks of the job. Our 'Enery simply made himself head-honcho of the brand new CHURCH OF ENGLAND, which fitted into the Reformation (rebellion against the Catholics) ever so nicely.

The Spanish, by this time, were getting far too big for their high-heeled boots, which really hacked off Henry's girl Elizabeth (from his headless ex-wife, Anne), who was now Queen. She sent her boyfriend, a certain wide-boy by the name of F. Drake, to sort 'em out, which he did...

In 1588, their Armada (a gaggle of huge Spanish galleons) arrived without so much as an invitation, only to be trashed by our nippy little ones (ha ha!). Lizzie then executed Mary, the Queen of the Scots, and died personally in 1603. This anti-Scottishism backfired as, later, we ended up being ruled by poor ex-Mary's little boy James: the little monkey thought kings should be allowed to do exactly as they pleased ('cos God had told him so). (He grew up to like men more than women, but we won't go into that now.)

A chap called Guy Fawkes would have none of this (or that!) and tried (unsuccessfully, unfortunately) to blow James and his friends (called Parliament) up, to prove it. He didn't die in vain, however, as his actions led to BONFIRE NIGHT.

47

America Goes Pure

As if America didn't have enough to worry about with the Spanish crawling all over it, in 1622 a bunch of English Puritans sailed across the Atlantic. On arrival, the self-styled Pilgrim Fathers tied up their little boat (the *Mayflower*) and called the bit that they'd tied it up to New England (original or what?) which it still is. They then proceeded to grow tobacco and drugs (hemp or hashish) which, when you think about it, doesn't sound that pure at all. The Red Indians (sorry, Native Americans) were still happily whooping, waving their tomahawks and smoke-signalling to each other all over the wide prairies, blissfully unaware of the problem these early settlers would one day become.

Europe Takes All

By this time the Europeans were having a right old time conquering and claiming as their own anywhere they bumped into. The Dutch took large chunks of Africa and the Portuguese took the rest. The French took a smallish bit of Canada (Quebec) and the British took the rest of it (before nicking the French bit as well). The British then took New Amsterdam off the Dutch and cheekily called it New York, while the French, battling away down south, took a large slice of boggy real estate and rather bizarrely called it Mississippi.

In 1707 the English patched up their old quarrel with the Scots and named the whole shooting match Great Britain (Wales and Ireland seem not to have had much say in the matter) just in time to have a brand new war with France. After the 100 Years War (which had got a bit boring) they decided this one would only go on for seven years (changing ends at three and a half). In 1758, our Captain Cook (later to become a travel agent), while cruising around the Indian Ocean minding his own business, had obviously high-tailed it so far from all this horrid fighting that he found himself sailing upside down. Whilst in this state he spied a little bit of land called ∀ITⱯꓤTꙄU∀ which he then declared 'discovered' and, of course, 'British'.

Back in America the immigrants had just woken up to the fact that all their spare, hard-earned cash was drifting back to the old country (Britain) in taxes, so, believing this to be a little unfair, showed us two fingers and declared they would go it alone. We British weren't impressed and tried to teach them a lesson. There then followed the War of Independence which ended with a home win for the new Yankees.

Science and Invention

In the same year (more or less) that Columbus discovered America, the Chinese discovered the toothbrush* and a Scotsman called Cor discovered whisky. This period was known as the Renaissance (rebirth), as the poor world had a lot to catch up on knowledge-wise after the Middle Ages. All that exploring, however, was very useful, as every day someone or other would arrive home with loads of weird animals and plants that they could study (or eat). Thanks to the Reformation it was becoming slightly easier for scientists (or 'natural philosophers') to investigate things and put forward new theories without having the church breathing down their necks and accusing them of heresy every five minutes. Having said that, that old Pole Copernicus (pronounced copper-knickers), who was the first to dare to suggest that the sun was the centre of the solar system instead of the Earth, got into deep trub with Him and his henchmen (later called the Inquisition).

Earth's Travels

It was an Italian called Galileo around the mid-sixteenth century, who, armed with a shiny new telescope, and a window in his bedroom ceiling, introduced EXPERIMENTATION and, so doing, laid the foundations for the sort of science we now know and

* About time too. The Romans had invented toothpaste centuries ago.

sometimes love. He proved conclusively that the Earth went round the sun, which was the centre of our solar system, but those head-in-the-sand Catholics wouldn't admit it till, would you believe, 1922.

Later, in 1665, a chap called Isaac Newton, following Galileo's principle of only believing what you can actually see yourself, discovered gravity and the laws of inertia (not to mention windfall apples) when he watched a Granny Smith fall from a tree in his mum's orchard. He was to become probably the most famous physicist in the whole history of the world (until Einstein pitched up).

Think Again

The science of Modern Philosophy, as we know it today, started with a French guy called Descartes, who claimed that 'he thought therefore he was', but I'm afraid that what he thought he was takes rather too long to explain... I think!

As for BOTANY, in 1580 it was discovered by Prospero Alpini that plants weren't just plants, but there were little boy plants and little girl plants who, given half a chance, would get together and produce baby plants, and Jan Baptiste van Helmont, who was into weighing trees, proved in 1648 that a willow tree does not gain weight simply from the soil (so what?).

Techno-babble

Technology hit one of its peaks in 1589 when Sir John Harrington, a godson of good Queen Beth, flushed with success, finally replaced the old hole-in-the-ground for the disposal of all things lavatorial. His water closet, generally accredited to Victorian Thomas Crapper (what a co-incidence) became the main topic of conversation amongst anyone rich or in desperate need of a ... Thomas.

... and Medicine

Medicine was to develop faster than all the other life sciences during this period. Anatomy was helped no end when people like Leonardo and his chums decided that the best way to find out how bodies (human or otherwise) worked, was to cut 'em up and pull 'em apart. Blood, for instance, was found to have a much more important function within our bodies than the rather spectacular mess it made when it escaped. A chap called Elshots in 1550 delighted in shooting various concoctions into the very veins that carried the stuff (blood, that is), to see if it made his patients feel better. Gradually loads of fab new diseases were identified like measles, malaria and syphilis but the treatment thereof often left rather a lot to be desired.

By the mid 1700s just about every bit of our bodies was under close scrutiny and, horror upon horrors, the first suggestions of slimming as a way of staying fit were put forward. At last someone started looking at the brain to see why it got poorly and in 1751 the first mental institution in England opened to care for the loony Londoners. These days it would be simpler and cheaper to open one for those who aren't.

You are Where you Live

But all sickness is largely linked to living conditions and

they were pretty jolly bad if you weren't a toff in the latter part of the eighteenth century. In 1776 a German called Hahnemann reckoned that you could be cured by things that grew in your average back garden (evening primrose oil, lavender, camomile etc.), and so invented HOMOEOPATHY. Eventually, however, they discovered that if this was true, there would be no money to be made, so insisted on recommending the obscurest plants possible.

... and Music

At the turn of the fifteenth century most ethnic music throughout the world was sounding much as it does today. Indian music sounded Indian, Chinese sounded Chinese, and Australian Aboriginal music sounded... appalling. Over in Europe, most people only listened to that rather doleful church music that you can still hear in huge cathedrals. Thomas Tallis was to become champion composer in England while over in Italy, Galileo's dad Vincenzo was plucking pleasantly at his lute and composing songs to play to his soon-to-be-star-struck baby (Twinkle, twinkle etc...?).

In 1553 some bright woodworker hacked out the first proper violin but it took another hundred or so years before Antonio Stradivari got it completely right (and another 300 before his instruments changed hands for telephone number cash). The violin's big brother, the cello, came along in 1572 and his even bigger brother, the double bass (as we know it), even later, in the early seventeenth century (which all sounds the wrong way round). Queen Elizabeth sent one of the first organs to the Sultan of Turkey (see early transplants) while the bane of all children (and their parents), the weedy recorder, became a craze in England in the early 1600s. The French horn (the one that looks like shiny intestines with a mouthpiece) joined the orchestra in 1664, but the piano proper wasn't wheeled on until 1709. Just in time for child prodigies like Mozart and Beethoven who, along with others like Vivaldi, Bach, Handel, Scarlatti, Haydn, were gurgling tunefully in their cots while the first of the

big boys of classical music, like Monteverdi and Purcell, became dead famous (instead of famous when dead). The eighteenth century was to be by far the most important century in the whole history of proper, grown-up music.

So what was Top of the Pops in the barren years leading up to that? The tune Greensleeves (di daa di daa di-di-daa di daa) was written in 1580 as a jingle for ice cream vans but, for obvious reasons, didn't really come into its own until the mid twentieth century. That miserable little number 'God Save the Queen' turned up a little later still.

Care to Dance?

And dance? Apart from the fairly new-fangled BALLET, what were the kids dancing to in those days? Well, over in France, the rather poncy French court was mincing about to the extremely sissy minuet. Just like the Twist in the 1960s, it rocketed round Europe like a good rude joke and could soon be seen at all the biggest and best balls (talking of rude jokes). Slightly later, in 1773, people started waltzing (*one*, two three, *one*, two, three) around Vienna, while in Spain the balefully boring Bolero (tump, tippity tump, tippity tump, tippity-tippity-tippity tump) was invented by a dancer called Carezo.

... and Art

After the appalling restrictions of the Middle Ages, painters and sculptors were falling over each other in a mad dash to slap paint on walls again. There were still loads of Madonnas with Childs (or is that children?) but, thankfully, they were now much better done, and even poor Jesus stopped looking like a reject from an inflatable doll factory. But the Renaissance in Italy was dominated by two giants – Leonardo da Vinci (again!) and Michelangelo, who broke new ground with whatever they touched (in Leo's case – Mona Lisa). Over in Holland, a rather posh chap called Peter Breugel painted happy common folk, while a right weirdo called Anonymous (that can't be right?) Bosch painted the most horrid pictures of where you would go if you didn't eat your greens (as well as inventing a host of domestic appliances).

Over in Japan, Ogota Korin united the Kano and Yamato Schools of Art just in time for their most famous painter Hokusai (swirly waves), who was born in 1760. In England, Hans Holbein (another Dutchman) had the rotten job of painting Henry VIII's fourth Missus, Anne of Cleves. Rotten, because she was nicknamed The Flemish Mare which, rumour had it, was actually an insult to lady horses. Old Henry really ought to have hung on for a few hundred years for George Stubbs, the English painter who could only do horses. Paul Rubens, on the other hand, had a high old time painting huge roly-poly, pink women with no clothes on (the women – not Paul!). In general, all the paintings from the hot countries, although still religious, were robust, colourful and jolly passionate, while all those from colder climes were rather tight, flat and super-realistic representations of everyday life.

... and lastly, Architecture

The Indians had the Taj Mahal, the Greeks had the Parthenon, the Americans had the wigwam and now it was our turn. Sir Christopher Wren, our best architect ever, built many of London's finest classical buildings (with a bit of baroque thrown in), like St Paul's Cathedral, St James's Piccadilly and St McDonald's Wandsworth.

All change

But by now, the British were just getting into their Industrial Revolution, a period that would see more changes than ever before...

THE LAST BIT

The Last Bit

. . . .

Around the time the 'modern world' began, a cocky little red-haired (no not Chris Evans) Corsican crowned himself Emperor Napoleon I of France and dissolved the Holy Roman Empire in favour of his own French one. Not bad for starters! Over on this side of the Channel, poor old George III had finally gone crackers and was replaced by the dreadful, foppish Prince Regent, who became George IV in 1811. He might have been a dead rotten king but (and no thanks to him) he did employ some sensational soldiers like Wellington, and super sailors like Nelson. Together they chased Napoleon all over the shop until in 1814 the French, who were losing gauche, droite et centre, realized poor Boney was losing the plot and banished the poor petit homme to Elba (an island in the middle of nowhere).

But you can't pin a good (if somewhat small) frog down and eventually he hopped back to France, proclaimed himself boss again and challenged Britain to a final punch-up at Waterloo (Platform 7). Wellington

NAPOLEON THE FIRST

(with a little help from the Russkies) finally gave him and his gutsy garçons the boot in 1815, and when Britain looked around after the war she realized that she had a jolly nice little Empire of her own, consisting of Canada, Australia (though mostly convicts), India, the Cape Colonies, Ceylon and Guyana. The French were somewhat less than amused and this time Napoleon was exiled to a dot of an island called St Helena (which wasn't even near the middle of nowhere).

Missionaries on a Mission

It was a time when pith-helmeted Christian missionaries were crawling all over distant lands trying to civilize natives who, up to that time, had been perfectly happy simply being uncivilized natives. China, however, would have none of it and outlawed Christian literature completely. In 1835 the hitherto boring Dutch, now co-incidentally called the Boers (meaning farmers) trekked all the way across South Africa setting up a vast colony known as the Transvaal, kindly letting the Zulus (who'd been living there quite happily for donkey's years) have a small bit of a large region called Natal to live in. Later, the even more boring Belgians nabbed another huge chunk of Africa and called it the Congo. The British, who wrote the book on greed, realized that if they didn't get their skates on there'd be none left. We had already grabbed Nigeria, Kenya, Nyasaland (now Malawi) and Rhodesia (now Zambia and Zimbabwe) and by 1902 we'd ousted the Boers and controlled the whole shooting match from South Africa right up to Cairo (where we shared the running of Egypt with the French).

In America, the Confederates and Yankees had been far too busy fighting amongst themselves (the American Civil War) to worry about such things, but when it was over they decided they'd be foolish not to snap up Alaska when the Russians decided to flog it, and shut down their own indigenous natives once and for all by making them live in small, but real-life, theme parks to play Red Indians in. Out East, the Chinese and the Japs finally stopped quarrelling in

1895 – Japan taking Formosa, and Korea becoming totally independent of both of 'em.

Queen Vic

England, at this time, had been ruled for ages by a funny little bug-eyed woman called Victoria (Queenie's great-grandmother), who never went out and wore black all the time (owing to the premature death of hubby Albert). She, with the help of a few clever ministers like Disraeli and Melbourne, underlined the Great in Britain, making us, and this almost defies belief nowadays, the most powerful nation in the whole world with an Empire that had grown to 240,000,000 people, of all shapes, sizes and hughs (or is that hues?).

Krauts About

But what about Germany? They weren't doing too badly in the old Empire-grasping game either, and were beginning to push their quite considerable weight around. Austria (where it seems just about every other bloke wore a big moustache and a pointy helmet) then upset Russia by jumping on Bosnia and Herzegovina (ever heard of them?). Then in 1914 it all went completely bonkers. Austria declared war on Serbia, Germany on Russia (and France) and Britain (so's not to feel left out)

declared war on just about everyone. At first this World War game looked like the worst idea we'd ever had, but thanks to our strapping sons – Canada, Australia, New Zealand, South Africa and India – who'd been standing just behind us, things began to go rather well, and by the time the Yanks came in it was game, set and match. True, we'd lost a million young men, but we'd won – what fun! – and the horrid Hun was well and truly done ... (for).

Here Comes Hitler

In 1919 the League of Nations was set up to make sure that a world war would never happen again, which it didn't. Well, not for fifteen years, when that funny little painter and decorator, with a stick-on moustache and badly fitting hair, a Mr Adolf – all reasonable jobs considered – Hitler, became chancellor (boss) of Germany. He wanted rid of anyone who wasn't blond and blue-eyed (even though he wasn't) which ruled out Jews, gypsies and just about anyone with a complexion darker than you'd get from a fortnight in Torremolinos. If this wasn't quite bad enough, he also made it fairly clear that he wouldn't be averse to the idea of Germany taking over the whole world.

Everyone now knows what a creep he turned out to be and how his rotten doings led to the Second World War in 1939. Our slightly prejudiced history of that war can be seen in the hundreds of black and white films that depict Britain and our allies (the Americans came in late... again) as clean-cut, jolly good fellows, and everyone on the other side as unshaven rotten bounders, so we won't go over all that. The game finally came to an end when America dropped far too big a bomb on the Japanese. It heralded the beginnings of the somewhat dubious NUCLEAR AGE. Maybe the only good effect of the horrendous scrap came in 1945 (the year it was all over) when the League of Nations was replaced by the United Nations to make sure it would never happen again... again!

But would it work this time? Read on.

The Cold War

The world was pretty shattered after this last crazy scrap and it took a long time to get back on its feet. Unfortunately, just like kids in a playground, everyone changed who they wanted to play with. The Germans, predictably, became our new mates, while the dear old Russkies, who'd helped fight the common foe, became our sworn enemies. We Westerners found that all-for-one, one-for all Communist stuff was simply not on for us survival-of-the-fittest capitalists. The stakes went through the roof, however, when everybody saw that the next war, if it ever happened, wasn't going to be fought with soppy guns and bayonets but with missiles carrying lethal bombs that seemed to work by splitting tiny atoms in half.

America and Russia, who were stockpiling these bombs as fast as they could make 'em, were really not getting on well at all, and even ended up not talking (hence the 'Cold' War) but spying on each other instead. Later China and Russia, who'd been all jolly good commies together, fell out. This was just as well for us, as the pact between America and Britain (Britain basically kissing their feet) could never have stood up to China and Russia combined if they'd turned any uglier. Germany and Japan, despite not having been that good at wars, turned out to be rather the opposite at peace, showing a clean pair of heels economically to the rest of us. Sad little Britain was left polishing its medals, as its standard of living plummeted like an absent-minded mountaineer. Sure we'd won, but we were left with an antiquated class system headed by fat capitalists who refused to invest in the very industry that had made them rich, and an antiquated royal family who didn't seem to notice.

America the Brave

America was riding high by the 1970s, and obviously saw themselves as the 'free' world's big, strong and unquestionably right brother, fighting fearlessly to protect the world from the dreaded communism. They barged into what was at the time a funny little war in Vietnam between two lots of people who looked to us to be exactly the same. Once stuck in, like wasps in a jam pot, the Yanks found they couldn't get out and thousands of young men were slaughtered for a cause that few could even get their heads round. So did the Americans learn to keep their noses out of other people's battles? Did they hell. Five minutes later (1983 to be precise) they were sticking their noses into the business of the natives on the tiny island of Grenada in the West Indies, but this time got away with it.

New Look Nelson

Over in Africa the real African Africans started to get back the countries that us whities had nicked off them all those years ago, but turned out to be about as competent as vegetarians running an abattoir when in power (a bit like any goverment, really). Down south, the newish white Africans hung on to their luxurious, 'let-the-blacks-eat-cake' regime until the bitter end. It was only when world pressure became too much that they were forced to release the very man that they'd kept banged up for years; the black Africans' hero, Nelson Mandela. He became the saviour and uniter of his people, forcing the whities to promise to behave themselves and share some of their wealth (even though many think they did it with their fingers crossed).

Most incredible of all, China and Russia, those great communist nations that had scared the pants off us all for so long, began to weaken at the knees. When Chairman Mao, who'd single-handedly returned his country to feudalism, died, his harsh regime died with him leaving a shell-shocked people (in very silly uniforms) hardly knowing what to do next. Later, to the amazement of the whole world, the giant and terrifying Russian bear suddenly swayed, tottered and crumbled into musty old bear-dust, leaving a country totally weak and totally divided (and deliciously vulnerable). The Cold War was won by the West without a single rocket being fired;

Communism as a practical concept had topped itself and Capitalism, for better or worse, had triumphed. Half the world was now laid open to be ravaged by the new peril — the dreaded multinational company. The new rulers were to be petrol, soft drink, sports-shoe and hamburger manufacturers. Big Mac Rules OK!

Britain Gets the 'Great' Back

Meanwhile, Britain had gone through its own mini-revolution. By the late 70s the Tories (who represent the middle classes and above) had finally squashed the Socialists (who represent the rest); and a fabulous leader, in the form of a grocer's daughter from Grantham, had given us a show-stopping economic concept. Why bother with all that hassle of actually manufacturing something when you could simply shift money around creaming profit from the transactions? She also proved what we all suspected, that hanging on to and multiplying your money if you already had it was far easier than trying to improve your lot (or loot) if you hadn't.

Great Britain, or should I say the mighty Queen Thatcher I (whose popularity was flagging), was also determined to show the world that we hadn't lost our touch and were still a mighty warrior nation. By pure chance we got the opportunity to practise on a little banana republic (Argentina) whose army were only just out of school uniform and hardly knew how to play soldiers. Better than that, the result hardly mattered, as the prize was only a couple of sheep-nibbled islands not much bigger than a supermarket car park, the location of which hardly anyone over here was sure of (and less people cared!). Predictably, just like the last couple of proper wars we'd fought – we won. The Falklands War had to be one of Britain's finest hours. Wasn't it?

When Empress Thatcher was deposed, we invented a new game called 'Let's-Find-the-Most-Unlikely-Person-to-be-Leader'. America thought it had won hands-down by voting in everyone from brazen cheats to peanut farmers, old cowboy-film stars to bad saxophone players.

(The only consolation was that that they did have a habit of shooting them at fairly regular intervals.) Britain, however, trumped them by choosing a circus acrobat's son who looked like a cross between a train-spotter and a gentlemen's outfitter. John Major, middle-aged, mid-grey and about as inspiring as a wet Sunday in March, symbolized the way European politics was going, his very lack of radical policies being his main qualification.

No More War?

And what about that dream that the United Nations would keep us all from tearing each other apart? As I write, the land formerly known as Yugoslavia (that slightly boring little ex-package holiday venue) has just finished ripping its own arms and legs off while the kindly UN forces (wearing those pretty blue berets) looked on, secure in the knowledge that by keeping the supply lines open, the natives wouldn't die hungry. In a world where every tragic sound bite has to fit on a T-shirt, ETHNIC CLEANSING became the 'in' term to hit the headlines. Innocent people were murdered willy-nilly, not for what they said but for some ancient bloodline that half of them had almost forgotten. Hitler, Satan bless 'im, no doubt smirks knowingly from his luxurious, if somewhat warm, underground apartment.

The Appliance of Science

What about the wonderful world of science and technology? Could it too affect the dull drab safe happy lives of Mr and Mrs Ordinary? The early nineteenth century had seen the beginning of what came to be known as the Industrial Revolution. Things that hadn't even been dreamed of, like steam power and electricity and chocolate Easter eggs, had become commonplace. Britons could chug along on the first trains while being photographed by the first photographers; soldiers could be killed by the first shells, while ships could be blown to smithereens by the first torpedoes; letters could be sent bearing the first stamps; the forerunners of teenagers (not seen till the 1950s) could dream about where to get the first Levi's jeans and chewing gum. A little later, Coca Cola could be glugged while listening to the first phonograph. In 1885, another German determined to conquer the modern world, Karl Benz, invented that scourge of all time, the motor car, but monumental as that turned out to be, the world had to wait until 1920 for that other great breakthrough in our everyday lives – the tea bag.

There were two major watersheds. The first came in 1835 when a young botanist/zoologist called Charles Darwin came home from an over-long boat trip in the Southern Seas where he'd been checking out plants and bugs (and the odd dusky maiden) to prove conclusively that we all came from the same primeval slime and that

Adam and Eve (and their pet serpent) were frauds. The second came in 1915 when a wacky-looking Swiss guy called Albert Einstein offered his Theory of Relativity to the world, which made the fairest stab to date at explaining the universe (and what really is at the end of the rainbow), though the problem came when he realized there was hardly anyone clever enough to understand what the hell he was going on about. Until, that is, Stephen Hawking came along and had another go in his *Brief History of Time* (which still nobody understood).

Telly Time

As we approach the last bit of the twentieth century, it's fair to say we're punch-drunk from the advances in science, but nobody could have imagined the consequences of two of the most important ones. If John Logie Baird had realized that by turning on the first telly he was to shrink the world to the point where everyone from Wigan to Woolabunga would be wearing the same T-shirts and trainers, drinking the same drinks, eating the same burgers, listening to the same pop music, worshipping the same stars, and laughing at the same jokes, he'd probably have taken it to bits and made something else. And if the guys who fiddled around with the first computers had sussed that in less than twenty years, the ******

things would be doing our thinking and even making our decisions for us, they'd have packed it in and gone out for a couple of beers instead.

Making Ourselves Better
Something small and nasty was discovered in the middle of the 19th century that was to shed light on the whole spectrum of reasons why we humans get sick. The germ turned out to be very bad for our health, until a French guy called Louis Pasteur found that if you introduce the

poor patient to the same germ or bacteria that's been making him poorly (called immunization), the little devils have a habit of killing each other, so making the said patient better. The rest of the century saw the discovery of quinine (for the treatment of malaria), chloroform (for the treatment of staying awake), cells (for the treatment of prisoners?) and a whole load of other fab new drugs like aspirin to treat various complaints from headaches to hepatitis.

X Marks the Spot

It was another French-person called Marie Curie who, in the early twentieth century, stumbled on the fact that natural radioactivity is rather good for the treatment of cancers and later used it to develop X-rays to look inside people. Unfortunately poor Marie fiddled around with these dangerous substances a little too often, and died in 1934 of leukaemia – the very disease she'd been trying to cure. Whoops!

By the 1920s, surgeons were able to do running repairs on the brain (neorosurgery) and an Englishman called Alexander Fleming found that the mould that had formed on the jelly (flavour unknown) that he'd accidentally left out in the lab proved to be brilliant in treating badly infected patients. He'd stumbled on penicillin (and a use for mouldy jelly).

Get Your Spare Parts Here

But the most spectacular medical developments came in the latter part of the twentieth century. Just about every part of the body from hearts to hips or livers to lungs could now be replaced like worn-out car parts. Lasers were used in surgery, making all that had gone before seem as clumsy as an arthritic concert pianist's version of the 'Flight of the Bumble Bee' (while wearing gardening gloves); whilst tiny little microscopic machines could now ferret around in our arteries, dusting and scrubbing and rendering them almost as good as new.

The discovery of DNA as a method of getting to the bottom of genetic disease, though relatively young, seems to offer a real possibility that soon kids won't have to blame their ancestors for all the things that are wrong with them, as genetic imperfections may be spotted *before* birth (too late, unfortunately, for Prince Charles's ears). Taking it further, if we take a lead from Jurassic Park, we might be able to re-create stars like Marilyn Monroe or Michael Jackson (in any colour) by simply nicking a sample of their DNA and reproducing it. Not strictly medicine, but loads of fun! Having said all this, there's still one major area that keeps the medical profession baffled, an area of research that has got no further since man began. When will they come up with a cure for my rapidly receding hairline?

Much More Music

In the nineteenth century, apart from a few crusty old folk songs, bawdy music-hall numbers, or the woeful works of Gilbert and Sullivan, the only music of any note (?) was of the still, rather grown-up, classical variety, usually written by long-dead (or dying) mid-Europeans, who'd either gone mad or who had something severely wrong with them. Beethoven, for instance, was stone deaf, which many would have thought might be somewhat of a drawback in the old composing biz.

Popular music for ordinary people really started in America. Negro slaves, while picking cotton, had tended

to cheer themselves up singing songs about waking up in the morning feeling... miserable. Then one of them must have saved up to buy a banjo (somewhat difficult to play, as the three pre-requisites of being a blues singer were that you were a) crippled, b) blind and c) an ex-slave). Stir in a few more plucky and blowy instruments, and you have the Jazz Age. Before long the American white man, realizing the popularity of this foot-tappin', finger-clickin', up-front black music (and realizing that there could be some serious loot to be made) started doing it bigger (if not better) – the Big-Band era was born. It had to happen. In the early 1920s, a guy called Lloyd Loar (see Great Men Who've Got a Lot to Answer For) went and set one of these instruments – the guitar – to electricity.

Teen Beat

Pop came along with the inspired invention of teenagers in the 50s, who instantly craved something their parents would disapprove of. Actually I'm surprised *everyone* didn't disapprove, as all that early stuff, by the likes of Bing Crosby, Doris Day and Frank Sinatra, now sounds positively geriatric to our sophisticated, if somewhat shell-shocked, modern ears. Proper rock and roll, which everyone over, say, thirty hated, had mutated from the up-tempo country music of the Southern States of America and finally hit Britain in 1954, in the form of Bill

Haley and the Comets. *Improper* rock and roll (called rhythm and blues) started with bands like the Rolling Stones who, God bless 'em, seem to be the only chaps intent on playing the same stuff till they collect their pensions (which, rumour has it, they may not need).

Black music constantly developed from blues to jazz to soul, to reggae, to house, to Jungle, to rap, to its present form – a kind of incomprehensible babble of black angriness. Instead of being blue about their lives, they're now hip-hopping mad! And now? All we seem to be left with are those groups of over-produced, over-choreographed, over-dressed pretty boys, who don't actually play anything but say far too much.

The Great Art See-Saw

Probably the greatest upset in the art world came about at the end of the nineteenth century when a gang of plucky Parisian painters tried to see if they could paint what they thought they saw rather than what they did see (you see?). These 'Impressionists', in turn, opened the door to a whole new bunch of painters led by a chap called Kandinsky who thought it quite cool to take this 'almost-reality' to a point where what they produced didn't look like anything at all. This 'abstract' art, in turn, opened the door to another lot of artists who thought it really flash to produce 'art' that not only didn't look like anything at all, but couldn't even be shown in a gallery, like fabric-wrapped buildings or huge piles of random rocks.

Bricked Up

All this nonsense – sorry – creativity was bubbling along quite nicely until perhaps the splendidest controversy of all occurred in 1982. The British public finally spotted the Great Emperor Art's lack of clothes when the Tate gallery bought 120 ordinary house-bricks for £8000 from a fast-talking brick-salesman-cum-sculptor called Carl Andre, who simply laid them in a two-deep pile on the floor. Despite the fuss, this kicked off an open season for anyone with an endless supply of quasi-intellectual spiel (or bricks) and a daft idea, to sell their wares to gullible dealers and galleries. If you really had been looking for something like Marc Quin's head, cast in his own blood, or canned poo from Manzoni to sit on your mantelpiece then for you art had finally reached its pinnacle. Eat your heart out, Leonardo.

AND NOW…

And Now . . .

. . . .

So what has this all led to? Where are we now? Where are we going? And what numbers are going to win the lottery next week?

This seems to be the state of play.

Politics
No change. Throughout the world we continue to vote in people who promise faithfully to make everything all right. When they fail to do it, we vote in others who promise even more faithfully to rectify the mistakes of the last lot (and make things even righter).

Religion
No change. The world's population pray to their individual gods who, like politicians, never seem to listen, but are nevertheless happy to sit by and watch the persecution of others who disagree.

Monarchy

No change. We continue to pay fortunes to keep an institution going that many think perpetuates the class system and should have ended with steam trains, outside toilets and hula hoops.

Medicine

No change. Doctors strive to prolong our lives, while we, through the conditions we create for ourselves — overpopulation, pollution and fast-food restaurants — contrive to shorten them.

Philosophy

No change. Clever people still churn out book after book to tell us what it's all about, while people who think they're even cleverer tell them they've got it all wrong.

Science
No change. As one breakthrough occurs to make our lives easier, a counterproductive side-effect from an earlier breakthrough is discovered to make it worse.

Music
No change. Kids, since history began, hate the music their parents like, and vice versa.

Art
No change. Most generations since cavemen think that the artists of the day are useless compared with those of yesterday (and are generally right).

Fashion

No change. Ever since time began, parents have been saying to their kids, 'Surely you don't think you're going out dressed like that?'

Literature: Nothing much until now, but recent massive breakthroughs in creative writing, culminating in this monumental work what I've just written!

Also by John Farman

ART: A COMPLETE AND UTTER HISTORY
(without the boring bits)

If you're one of those people who think Caravaggio is an Italian motor home, or that Botticelli is some kind of pasta, that Gilbert and George were a sixties pop group, and you're baffled by Art in general, then fear not. You too can be an expert! John Farman continues to debunk the establishment: from the days before paint was invented, the History of Art makes its doomed way towards the present day and a pile of bricks in the Tate Gallery...

'Brilliantly funny' *Pissarro*

'I knew it would come to this' *Leonardo*

'It's unreal' *Salvador Dalí*

Also by John Farman

A PHENOMENALLY PHRANK
HISTORY OF PHILOSOPHY
(without the poncy bits)

This superbly succinct and absolutely jargon-free summary provides a Who They Were and What They Thought guide to Everything You Ever Needed To Know About Western Philosophy. It is also the only philosophy book you ever read that will make you laugh.

John Farman didn't know his neo-realism from his Nietzsche when he started this book. He can now hold his own (and often does) quite convincingly for seconds at a time, in any deep and meaningful conversation about life, the universe, and all that.

'A philosopher's nightmare' *Freud*

'Having read this, I *think* I'm glad I'm *not* any more' *Descartes*